W9-DFY-366

# How to Draw
# DOLPHINS
## and Other Sea Creatures

# Peter Gray

## PowerKiDS
### press.

Published in 2014 by The Rosen Publishing Group, Inc.
29 East 21st Street, New York, NY 10010

Illustrations: © Peter Gray
Editors: Joe Harris and Nicola Barber
U.S. Editor: Joshua Shadowens
Design: sprout.uk.com
Cover design: sprout.uk.com

Library of Congress Cataloging-in-Publication Data

Gray, Peter, 1969–
   How to draw dolphins and other sea creatures / by Peter Gray.
      pages cm. —  (How to draw animals)
   Includes index.
   ISBN 978-1-4777-1302-0 (library binding) — ISBN 978-1-4777-1415-7 (pbk.) — ISBN 978-1-4777-1416-4 (6-pack)
   1.  Marine animals in art—Juvenile literature. 2.  Drawing—Technique—Juvenile literature.  I. Title.
   NC781.G73 2014
   743.6—dc23
                                        2013004303

Printed in China

SL002688US

CPSIA Compliance Information: Batch #AS3102PK: For Further Information contact Rosen Publishing, New York, New York at 1-800-237-9932

# CONTENTS

The Basics. . . . . . . . . . . . . . . . 4

Tips and Tricks . . . . . . . . . . . 6

Dolphin . . . . . . . . . . . . . . . . 8

Sea Lion . . . . . . . . . . . . . . 14

Seahorse. . . . . . . . . . . . . . 18

Great White Shark. . . . . . . 22

Underwater Scene. . . . . . . 26

Glossary . . . . . . . . . . . . . . 32

Further Reading. . . . . . . . . . . 32

Websites . . . . . . . . . . . . . . . . 32

Index . . . . . . . . . . . . . . . 32

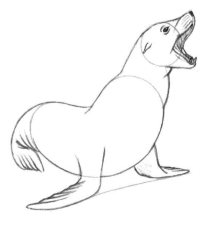

# THE BASICS

## DRAWING

**Start your drawings with simple guidelines before fleshing them out with detail.**

Build up the general shape of your subject with guidelines. I have drawn the guidelines heavily to make them easy to follow, but you should work faintly with a hard pencil.

**Guidelines**

**Detail**

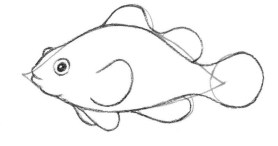

Use a softer pencil to develop the character and details. You may find that you do not follow the guidelines exactly in places. That's fine—they are only a rough guide.

**Shading and texture**

Carefully erase the guidelines and mistakes. Then add shading and texture with a soft pencil.

## INKING

**For a bold look, go over the outlines with ink. Wait for the ink to dry thoroughly, then erase all the pencil marks.**

**Felt-tip pen outlines**

The easiest inking method is to use a felt-tip pen. If you plan to add paint later on, make sure your pen is waterproof.

**Brush outlines**

For a more graceful effect, use a fine-tipped watercolor brush dipped in ink.

# COLORING

Although I use watercolors in this book, the main principles are the same for any materials— start with the shading, then add in markings and textures, and finally, work your main colors over the top.

**Felt-tip coloring**

Felt-tip pens produce bright, vibrant colors. Work quickly so that the pen strokes do not remain visible.

**Colored pencils**

Colored pencils are the easiest coloring tools to use, but you have to take great care to blend the colors to achieve a good finish.

**Watercolors**

The subtlest effects can be achieved with watercolor paints. It is best to buy watercolor paints as a set of solid blocks that you wet with a brush. Mix the colors in a palette or on an old white plate.

# TIPS AND TRICKS

## TEETH

Different marine creatures have very differently shaped teeth. Here are some tips to help you draw them. A shark's teeth are especially impressive.

### SHARK TEETH

The shark's upper teeth are simple triangles.

Start with a basic head and mouth shape.

Mark the lines of the gums and a line to indicate the length of the upper teeth.

Mark in the upper teeth. The lower teeth curve inward, and there are rows of new teeth growing up behind the front set.

### DOLPHIN TEETH

The dolphin's teeth are small and neat.

For the basic head shape, note that the dolphin's lower jaw is slightly longer than its upper jaw.

Draw simple lines to guide you for the straight rows of tiny teeth.

The teeth are arranged in orderly rows around the inside of the snout.

### SEA LION TEETH

The sea lion's lower canines are its most noticeable teeth.

Draw the basic head and mouth shape.

Draw the large lower **canines** and the gum lines.

The sea lion's lower and upper canines are surrounded by neat rows of pointed teeth.

# DOLPHIN SHAPES

Here are some tips for drawing a dolphin from several different viewpoints.

The same approach can be used for many other creatures found in the oceans. The details and **proportions** may vary, but they can be drawn using the same basic shapes.

This diagram shows the dolphin side-on. The shape can be broken down into a long oval and a pointed tail, with the nose and fins added on.

Seen from the front, the basic shape is little more than a circle. It is difficult to make this look real.

A better angle of view shows the front and side at the same time. It is a lot like the side-on view, except that the oval and tail are more squashed.

This is similar to the previous viewpoint, but the dolphin appears to be closer. The face is larger and the tail smaller.

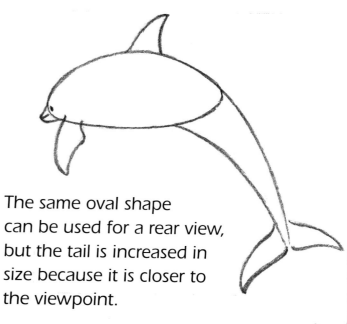

The same oval shape can be used for a rear view, but the tail is increased in size because it is closer to the viewpoint.

# DOLPHIN

Dolphins live in the world's warmer seas and oceans, usually in groups known as "pods." These are bottlenose dolphins—they are called that because their long snouts look a little bit like bottles! They can vary in color from light bluish gray to almost black.

**1** I decided to draw a pair of dolphins swimming together. You can, of course, choose to draw only one. The body shape of the main dolphin is two curves meeting at a broadly rounded head. The other dolphin is a long oval with a separate tail.

**2** Add the shapes of the snouts, one closed and the other open. The tail fins start as simple triangles. Make sure these triangles fit **symmetrically** onto the body.

**3** Draw the back fins and flippers. Note that the back fins sit to the rear of the bodies. Add mouth openings that extend into the head—these will help you to position the eyes.

**4** Shape the tail fins neatly within the triangles. Then work on the other fins, rounding off the corners and blending them smoothly into the bodies. Complete the snout shapes with curved lines where the upper jaw joins the head.

**5** Make sure your drawings are sleek and streamlined, and erase any confusing guidelines. Because the shapes of these animals are fairly simple, you need to be careful with every outline.

**6** For the inking stage, try to ink each part of your drawing with continuous, unbroken lines. Use a fine but well-loaded brush, so that the ink doesn't run out halfway along a graceful curve. Make the outline slightly broader on the shaded undersides and finer along the upper surfaces.

**7** Even simple coloring like that of the dolphin requires several stages to be really effective. Work on the shading first. For this picture, I used a blue-gray color. Before each section dried, I softened the edges with a wet brush to blend the dark parts into the light, to suggest smoothly rounded bodies.

# DOLPHIN SENSES

Dolphins are highly intelligent creatures. When they are hunting, they make clicking sounds and then listen for the echo of the sound as it bounces back. The time it takes for the sound to return tells the dolphin how far away its prey is. This is called echolocation. Dolphins also "talk" to each other with a wide range of whistles and other sounds.

ANIMAL FACTS

**8** Now add the plain gray coloring. For this, I mixed some golden brown into the gray. Mix up plenty of paint so you don't run out halfway through the painting. I painted this layer in swift, broad strokes and softened the bottom edges to blend into the pale undersides.

**9** To bring some roundness to the shapes of the dolphins, and to show where the light falls, I lightened the upper surfaces. I used a soft, damp brush to moisten the paint and lift it off the surface, cleaning the brush frequently.

**10** For the final touches, I diluted white ink with water to pick out the delicate highlights on the upper parts and to neaten up the mouth and eye areas. Then I mixed some blue into the white ink to paint some fine strips of color on the dolphins' undersides.

# SEA LION

Sea lions live in water and on land—they are powerful swimmers, and they are also able to move easily on all fours on dry land. Together with fur seals they form the group of "eared seals," because they have tiny earflaps on the outsides of their heads.

**1** For this upright pose, the sea lion's back is bent in the middle. Draw the head as a small circle, separated from the body.

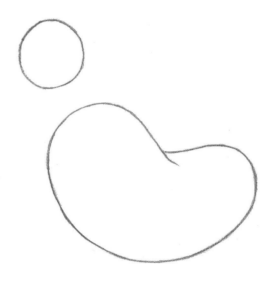

**2** Connect the head to the body with curves that bulge out on either side. Extend the rear end with a rounded line that flows smoothly into the back. To place the front flippers squarely on the ground, draw a sloping line to mark their front edges, then draw the flippers to meet this line.

# CALIFORNIA SEA LION

The fastest of all the different types of sea lion is the California sea lion. It lives along the west coast of North America. It can reach speeds of up to 25 miles per hour (40 kilometers per hour) in the water. Beneath its sleek skin, it has a thick layer of blubber (fat) to keep it warm in the chilly waters of the Pacific Ocean.

ANIMAL FACTS

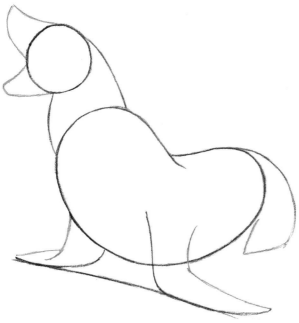

**3** Finish the flipper shapes both at the front and the back. Then work on the outline of the **muzzle** and the wide-open mouth.

**4** Complete the mouth inside the muzzle with the lower canine teeth. Add whiskers and an eye. Then add some detail to the flippers.

**5** Work on the outlines, making sure all the lines are graceful and that the sea lion looks like it is standing on a flat surface. Add the little earflap at this stage.

**6** The inking is fairly simple, but be careful to make all the lines smooth and streamlined. Turn the page regularly so that your hand can follow its natural movement.

**7** For the coloring, I used many of the same techniques described on pages 11 to 13. To create the mottled effect on the sea lion's chest, I painted dots of reddish brown onto a creamy color while the paint was still wet, so that the two colors ran into each other. This technique is known as wet-on-wet. I used broad, white highlights to create an effect of light bouncing off smooth, wet skin.

# SEAHORSE

These strange little creatures look like miniature horses—that's where their name comes from. However, they are actually bony fish. They swim upright in some of the world's warm seas and oceans by fluttering the small fins on their backs. To rest, they attach themselves to corals or seagrasses with their long, spiral tails.

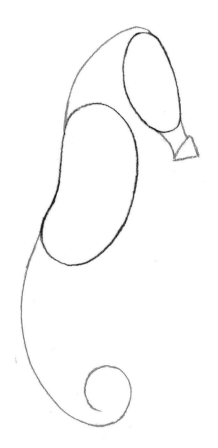

**1** Start the seahorse's long head and body with two slightly squashed ovals. The head should be fairly flat on top and more rounded underneath. The body dips in at the back, in a bean shape.

**2** Connect the two ovals with an arching line for the outside of the neck. The tail begins as a long curve that runs from the back and ends in a loose spiral. Add in the triangular nose part.

# SEAHORSE SNACKS

Seahorses use their long snouts to suck in tiny sea creatures for food. They have no teeth and no stomach! This means that seahorses must feed almost constantly in order to process enough food to keep them alive.

**ANIMAL FACTS**

**3** Draw the inside line of the tail, which forms a tight spiral at the end. Add facial features and fins around the jawline and in the middle of the back.

**4** Mark some guidelines for the ridges on the seahorse's body. Be careful to make them regular in size on the body and smaller as you work down the tail.

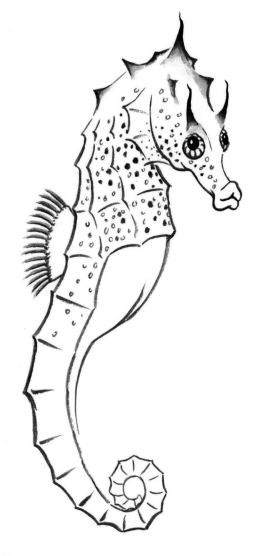

**5** Now you can refine your drawing, adding detail and texture to the guidelines. Work on the ridges of the body to give them some depth. Then spend some time working on the features of the face and the back fin.

**6** For such a delicate and colorful creature, I chose a warm red-brown color for the inking stage. I used black ink for the eyes and the tips of the horns. I also added some small dots and circles around the face and chest.

**7** Like many fish, seahorses come in a remarkable range of colors and markings. Some are dull brown and gray, but I chose a more colorful example. I used orange and yellow, blending into a greenish tint around the face. White highlights help to bring out the various ridges and bumps on the seahorse's body.

# GREAT WHITE SHARK

The great white shark is the world's largest **predatory** fish. It hunts other fish, sea lions, seals, and dolphins, turtles, and seabirds. Its body is shaped for speedy swimming, and its gray coloring makes it hard to spot against a rocky seabed. It gets its name from its white underside.

**1** This first shape is very simple, but it must be very accurately drawn if you want a fearsome-looking shark!

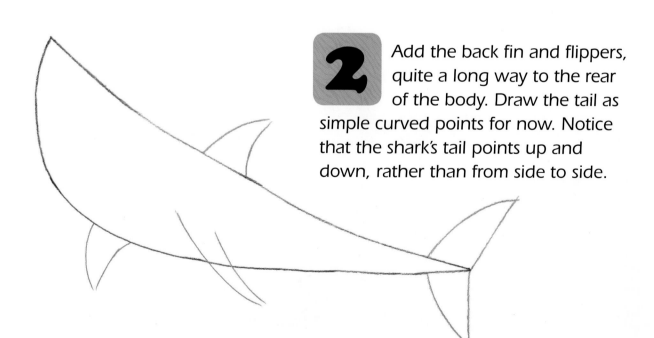

**2** Add the back fin and flippers, quite a long way to the rear of the body. Draw the tail as simple curved points for now. Notice that the shark's tail points up and down, rather than from side to side.

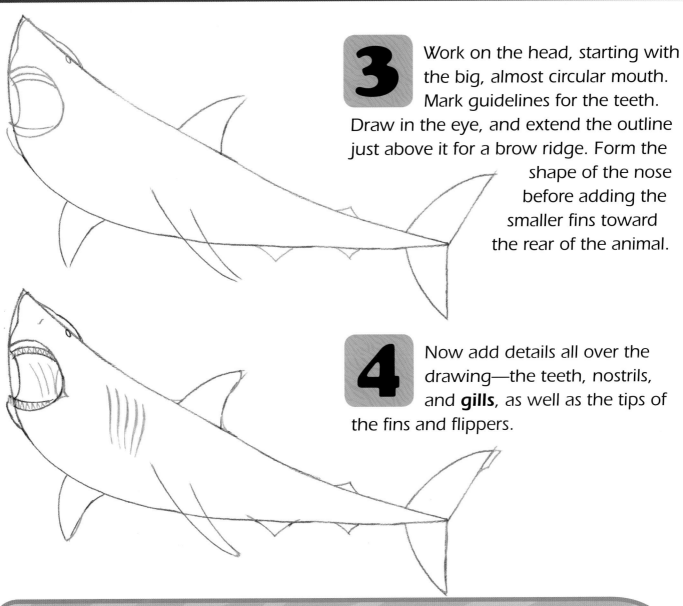

**3** Work on the head, starting with the big, almost circular mouth. Mark guidelines for the teeth. Draw in the eye, and extend the outline just above it for a brow ridge. Form the shape of the nose before adding the smaller fins toward the rear of the animal.

**4** Now add details all over the drawing—the teeth, nostrils, and **gills**, as well as the tips of the fins and flippers.

# SHARK SIZES

Female great white sharks are usually bigger than the males. On average, they grow up to 15 feet (4.6 meters) long, but some sharks reach lengths of around 20 feet (6 meters). They can live for more than 30 years.

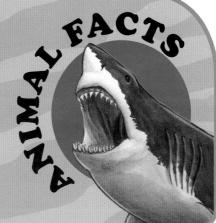

ANIMAL FACTS

**5** You may need to sharpen your pencil before working on the pointed teeth! Add a touch of simple shading inside the mouth. As you work over the outlines, never be afraid to redo any parts of the drawing that look clumsy or wrong.

**6** For the inking stage, work with long fine strokes, paying special attention to the pointed ends of the fins and flippers. You might need to switch to a very fine pen to ink in the teeth.

**7** Although the true color of the underside of this shark is white, it needs to be shaded to suit the light source and surroundings. With the light coming from above, the underside is in shadow, so I painted this part with a purple-gray color. The color of the surrounding sea gives a blue sheen to the areas of lesser shade. The color of the mouth is important, too. Make it very slightly pink inside and richer in color around the teeth.

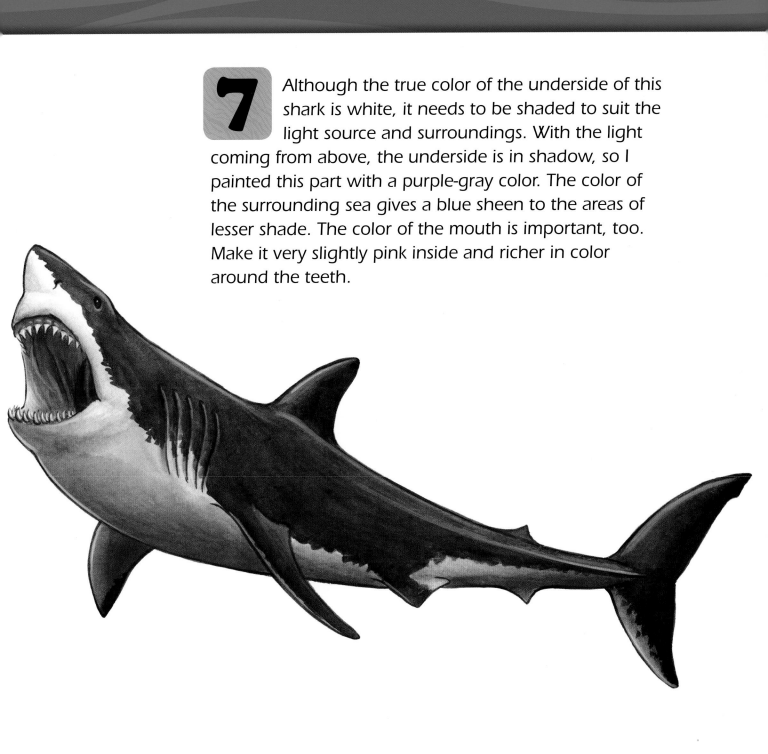

# UNDERWATER SCENE

Now it's time to bring together the skills you have learned in this book to place your sea creatures against a suitable background. I decided to use an underwater scene that shows two dolphins swimming near a sunken shipwreck.

**1** I found lots of photographs of underwater scenes and started to think about a suitable setting. Working roughly on a small sheet of paper, I arranged the boat so that it echoes the shape of the leading dolphin and makes a sweeping curve through the picture.

**2** To figure out the shading and coloring, I washed some colors directly onto my pencil rough. I used purply blue for the shadow areas and deep water, then yellows, oranges, and greens for the coral, plants, and the rusty shipwreck. For the open water, I used a paler turquoise blue.

**3** Still working on my color rough, I strengthened the outlines and shadows of the dolphins, coral, and plants in the **foreground** with black ink and more purply-blue paint. I also added some highlights with white ink. To make the scene livelier, I worked in a number of small fish, some as distant, dark shapes and some in bright yellow in the foreground.

**4** On a large sheet of good paper, I mapped out the basic shapes of the drawing in pencil. At this stage, I decided to add some extra dolphins in the background.

**5** I worked up the details of the drawing over the rough guidelines, still in pencil. I didn't put in too much detail for the corals and weeds, since this can be added directly at the inking stage.

**6** For the inking, I mainly used blue ink to create the effect of looking through water. I made the outlines more and more dark toward the foreground, switching to black ink for the corals and plants and the nearest dolphin. Once the ink was dry, I erased all the pencil marks.

**7** Before applying any color, I painted all the shading and shadow areas. I used pale, diluted blue for the distant parts, darker blue in the middle ground, and black shadows in the foreground.

**8** To color the scene, I started by filling in the solid blue of the sea, darker at the sea floor and paler toward the surface. I then roughly colored all the other parts with browns, oranges, and greens, then used gray for the dolphins. Once all the paper was covered, I mixed white ink into the colors to pick out textures and highlight edges. I also used a few touches of neat white ink for highlights in the foreground.

# GLOSSARY

**canines** (KAY-nyns) Long, pointed teeth, like fangs.

**foreground** (for-GROWND) The front of a picture.

**gills** (GILZ) The slits that allow a shark to "breathe."

**muzzle** (MUH-zel) The nose and mouth of an animal.

**predatory** (PREH-duh-tor-ee) Describes an animal that hunts other animals for food.

**proportions** (pruh-POR-shunz) Relating the size of one thing to another.

**symmetrically** (sih-MEH-trih-kul-lee) The same on both sides of a center point or line.

# WEBSITES

Due to the changing nature of Internet links, PowerKids Press has developed an online list of websites related to the subject of this book. This site is updated regularly. Please use this link to access the list:

**www.powerkidslinks.com/HTDA/sea**

# FURTHER READING

Ames, Lee J. and Warren Budd. *Draw 50 Sharks, Whales, and Other Sea Creatures.* New York: Watson-Guptill, 2012.

Carney, Elizabeth. *Everything Dolphins.* Washington D.C.: National Geographic Kids, 2012.

Walter Foster Creative Team. *All About Drawing Sea Creatures & Animals.* Laguna Hills, CA: Walter Foster, 2005.

# INDEX

bottlenose dolphins 8–13, 26–31

California sea lion 15

coloring 5, 11–13, 17, 21, 25, 27, 30–31

dolphins 6, 7, 8–13, 26–31

fish 4–5, 6, 18–21, 22–25

great white shark 6, 22–25

inking 4, 10, 16, 20, 24, 27, 29

sea lions 6, 14–17

seahorses 18–21

sharks 6, 22–25

teeth 6, 15, 23, 24, 25